THE BOY IN THE GARDEN

Written and illustrated by

ALLEN SAY

HOUGHTON MIFFLIN BOOKS FOR CHILDREN

Houghton Mifflin Harcourt

Boston New York 2010

To Miki

Houghton Mifflin Books for Children is an imprint of
Houghton Mifflin Harcourt Publishing Company.

www.hmhbooks.com

The text of this book is set in Garamond.
The illustrations are done in watercolor.

Library of Congress Cataloging-in-Publication Data
Say, Allen.
The boy in the garden / written and illustrated by Allen Say.
p. cm.
Summary: After Jiro encounters a life-like garden statue of a tall bird, he falls asleep
and dreams of the story his mother once told him about a grateful crane.
ISBN 978-0-547-21410-8
[1. Dreams—Fiction. 2. Cranes (Birds)—Fiction. 3. Japan—Fiction.] I. Title.
PZ7.S2744Bo 2010
[E]—dc22
2009046722

Printed in Singapore
TWP 10 9 8 7 6 5 4 3 2 1
4500232239

The Grateful Crane

Once, in old Japan, a young woodcutter lived alone in a little cottage. One winter day he found a crane struggling in a snare and set it free. Late that night a beautiful woman knocked on his door; she was lost in the snowstorm, and he gladly gave her shelter. She stayed for several days, and some time later they were married. They were happy, but very poor.

The wife saw an old loom in the back room and said she would weave something they could sell. But before she began, she made her husband promise not to peek while she worked. For three days and three nights he heard the creaking and tapping of the loom, but he did not peek. On the fourth morning, the wife, pale and unsteady on her feet, handed him a fold of the most beautiful cloth he had ever seen. He took it to town and sold it to a rich merchant for a handful of gold coins. The two lived in peace and happiness until they were poor again.

So the wife made another fold of cloth more beautiful than the one before. The husband sold it for a bagful of gold coins. They were rich. But the woodcutter wanted to be richer, and he asked the wife to weave yet one more piece of cloth. She shook her head, but he pleaded with her until she agreed wearily. Again, she asked him not to look and disappeared into the back room.

On the fourth night, he was overcome with curiosity and peeked. He saw a crane at work, plucking its gleaming feathers and feeding them to the loom. He cried out, and at once the bird became his wife again.

"I am the crane whose life you saved," she said. "Ever grateful, I changed into a woman and became your wife. But now that you have broken your promise, I can no longer be a woman."

She turned back into a great bird and flew away.

On the third day of January, father and son went to wish Mr. Ozu a happy new year.

"We are in a very famous garden," said Father. "And there are many treasures in the house, so mind your manners."

The boy did not hear him.

Mr. Ozu gave the boy a New Year's present—an envelope no bigger than a name card. The boy knew there was money inside, but it was impolite to open it until he got home. So he smiled his thanks and looked out the window while the grownups talked. When he wandered out of the room, no one noticed.

The boy put on his coat and went outside. From behind a big rock, he peeked at a tall bird standing in the garden.

He took a slow step and stopped. He took another step and the stones crunched beneath his feet.

The bird did not move.

Slowly he crept on the noisy stones, holding his breath, eyes fixed on the bird. One step away, he raised his arms . . .

"Ha, ha, ha!" bursts of laughter rang out.

The boy froze.

"That's only a statue, Jiro!" Father called from the house.

"How charming," Mr. Ozu said. The two men laughed together.

The boy ran from the bronze crane.

He ran until he could not see the house. Still, laughter rang in his ears.

"They were watching me the whole time," he said, panting. "Papa thinks I'm foolish and Mr. Ozu thinks I'm silly . . . I was only pretending. I was thinking about the 'Grateful Crane' story that Mama read to me . . . the crane that the woodcutter saved from the trap."

As he walked, he saw a small cottage.

"It's the woodcutter's house!" he said excitedly. "And he forgot to close the door."

Jiro peeked in shyly and found the house was empty.

Sniffing the air, he took off his shoes and crawled in. A folded kimono lay by the fire. "It's too small for a grownup," he said. "Maybe the woodcutter has a son."

Jiro took off his coat and tried on the kimono. It was just his size. Mother usually had to help him with the obi, but this one he could tie behind his back. Suddenly, he felt older.

Then Jiro heard a rustling sound outside.

"The woodcutter is home!"

Jiro slid the door open, ready to apologize for being in the house. But instead of the woodcutter, a tall woman stood on the doorstep.

"Welcome, Jiro-san," she said, and bowed.

The boy stared. "How did you know my name?"

The woman smiled.

"Are y-you the . . ." he stammered. "Aren't you supposed to be lost in the snowstorm? You're supposed to come later—"

"It is long past your suppertime." She folded the umbrella and closed the door. "Come, you must be very hungry."

The woman served him a bowl of soup and then covered the pot with a lid. "I am not hungry," she explained.

Jiro put the bowl down. "You're the Crane Woman, aren't you?" he asked.

The woman only smiled.

"You were in the bird statue and pretending, weren't you? You saw me coming here, so you opened the door and put the kimono out. But how did you get here before I did?" Jiro asked.

"My, you have a wonderful imagination." The woman laughed softly. "Now eat your soup before it gets cold."

The next morning, Jiro asked the woman for a piece of rope.

"The snow is too deep to play in," she told him.

"I'll go to the forest and gather firewood," he answered.

"There is no need for you to go out. I will do a little work," she said.

"No!" he cried, and ran from the house.

From the edge of the forest, Jiro looked back and waved to the woman. "I'm like Papa going to work in the morning," he thought. "I'm the woodcutter. I'll sell firewood and buy things to eat."

All day he searched in the forest and found not even a twig.

"The Crane Woman is hungry," he told himself. "I have to find something I can sell." Suddenly he stopped and shouted, "There's money in that envelope from Mr. Ozu!"

He rushed out of the forest and saw the cottage with glowing windows. Even before he had reached the house, the woman opened the door.

"Welcome back," she said.

"Where is the village?" the boy asked. "I can buy something to eat."

"The village is far, and nothing is open at this hour. Come—sit by the fire and I will do a little weaving."

"No!" Jiro cried.

The woman took a step toward the tattered door.

"Don't go in there," Jiro pleaded.

"It will only be for a while, but you must promise not to peek while I work."

"No, I'll never peek. Never! But don't go! You'll be a—"

She disappeared into the dark room.

Soon he heard the creaking and tapping of the loom working.

"Stop!" he shouted.

The creaking went on—the creaking of a door opening. Then he heard voices.

"Wake up, son. You're having a bad dream," Father called from the doorway.

Jiro sat up and rubbed his eyes.

"A charming boy," Mr. Ozu laughed. "Naps in the teahouse, like a cat."

Father chuckled, too. "Come, Jiro. It's time to go home."

As they left the villa, Father said, "It was easy to find you, you were shouting so." Jiro did not answer. Father turned to where the boy was looking and stopped.

"You know, son, for a moment that crane looked real."

"It's just a statue, Papa."

"And a fine statue, too," Father said.

Jiro only smiled.

They were home by supper, and by the time the moon rose
above the garden of Mr. Ozu, Jiro was fast asleep in his own bed.